# THE BIGGEST DINOSAURS

Written and illustrated by
## Michael Berenstain

A GOLDEN BOOK • NEW YORK
Western Publishing Company, Inc., Racine, Wisconsin 53404

Long, long ago dinosaurs ruled the world.
Some dinosaurs were small, and others were
big. But some dinosaurs were very, *very* big.

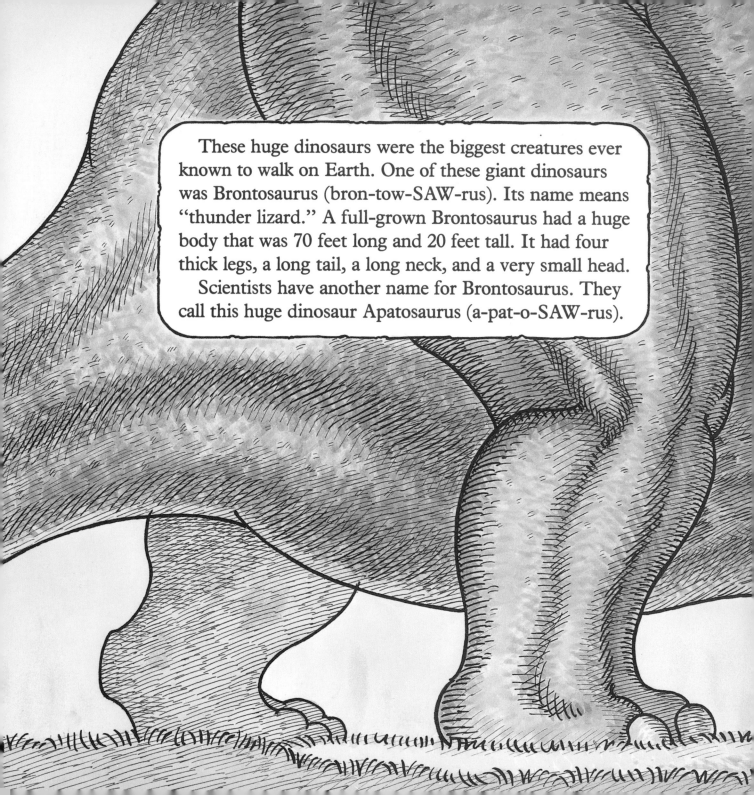

These huge dinosaurs were the biggest creatures ever known to walk on Earth. One of these giant dinosaurs was Brontosaurus (bron-tow-SAW-rus). Its name means "thunder lizard." A full-grown Brontosaurus had a huge body that was 70 feet long and 20 feet tall. It had four thick legs, a long tail, a long neck, and a very small head.

Scientists have another name for Brontosaurus. They call this huge dinosaur Apatosaurus (a-pat-o-SAW-rus).

Many of the biggest dinosaurs were plant-eaters. Brontosaurus may have eaten the tops of trees, raking in leaves with its long, thin teeth.

Brontosaurus probably didn't chew its food. It may have swallowed it whole, just like a bird. A bird swallows gravel and uses it to grind up food inside its body. Perhaps Brontosaurus did the same when it swallowed plants close to the ground. But instead of gravel, it would have swallowed whole rocks!

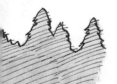

Brontosaurus probably wasn't very smart. It didn't have to be. Because of its huge size, it must have had very few enemies.

Allosaurus, a great meat-eating dinosaur, might have tried to catch and eat Brontosaurus.

But a full-grown Brontosaurus could have used its long, heavy tail and sharp thumb-claws to defend itself.

Things were very different for a baby
Brontosaurus. Its world was full of danger.

To protect her young, the mother Brontosaurus laid her eggs in large mud nests and watched over them until they hatched.

Brontosaurus probably lived in herds the way elephants do today. Their young would have stayed in the middle of the herds for safety. And, like elephants, Brontosaurus may have wallowed in pools and swamps to keep cool.

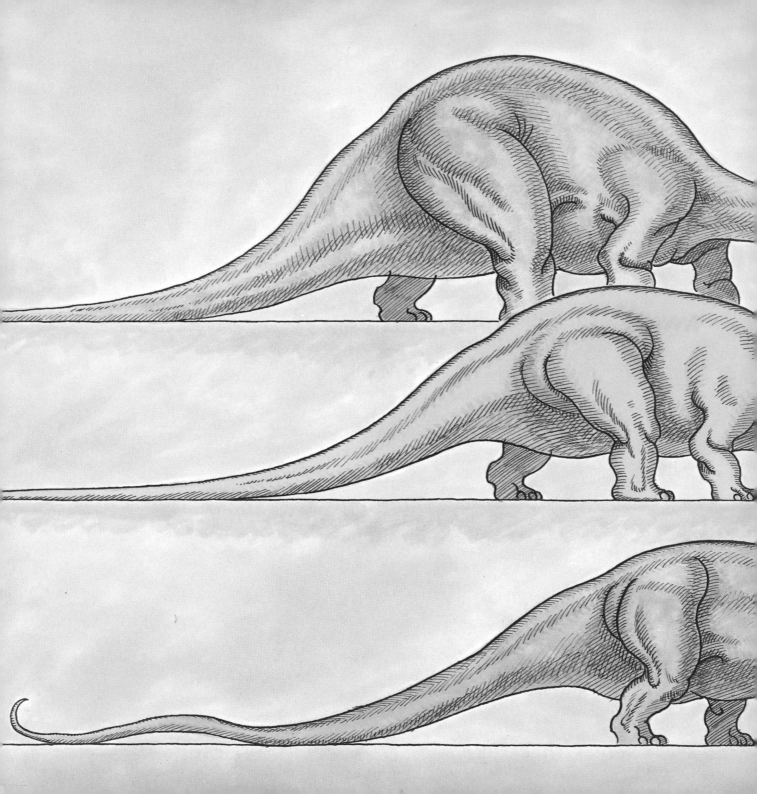

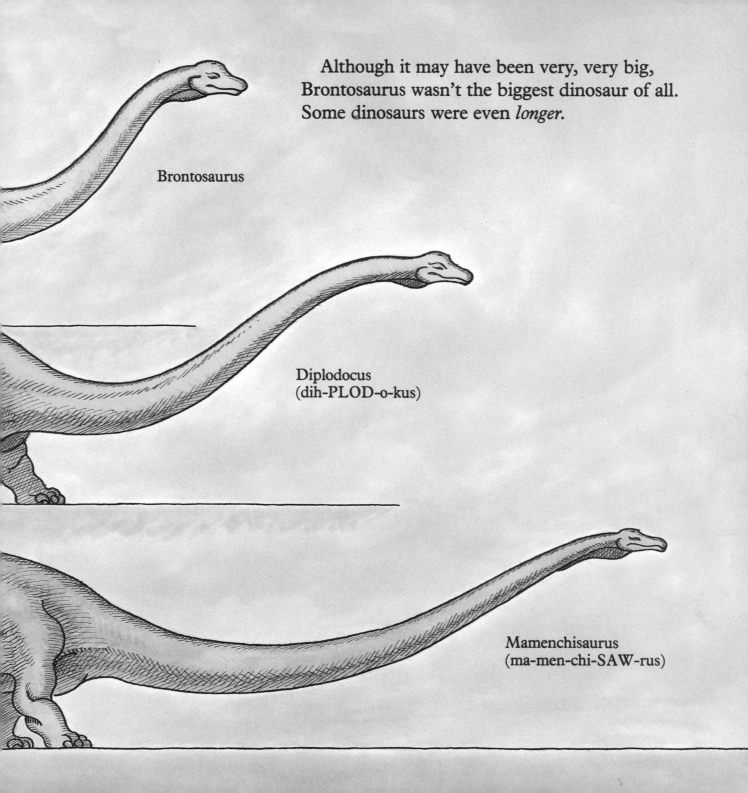

Although it may have been very, very big,
Brontosaurus wasn't the biggest dinosaur of all.
Some dinosaurs were even *longer*.

Brontosaurus

Diplodocus
(dih-PLOD-o-kus)

Mamenchisaurus
(ma-men-chi-SAW-rus)

And some dinosaurs were *taller*.

Brachiosaurus
(brack-ee-o-SAW-rus)

Brontosaurus

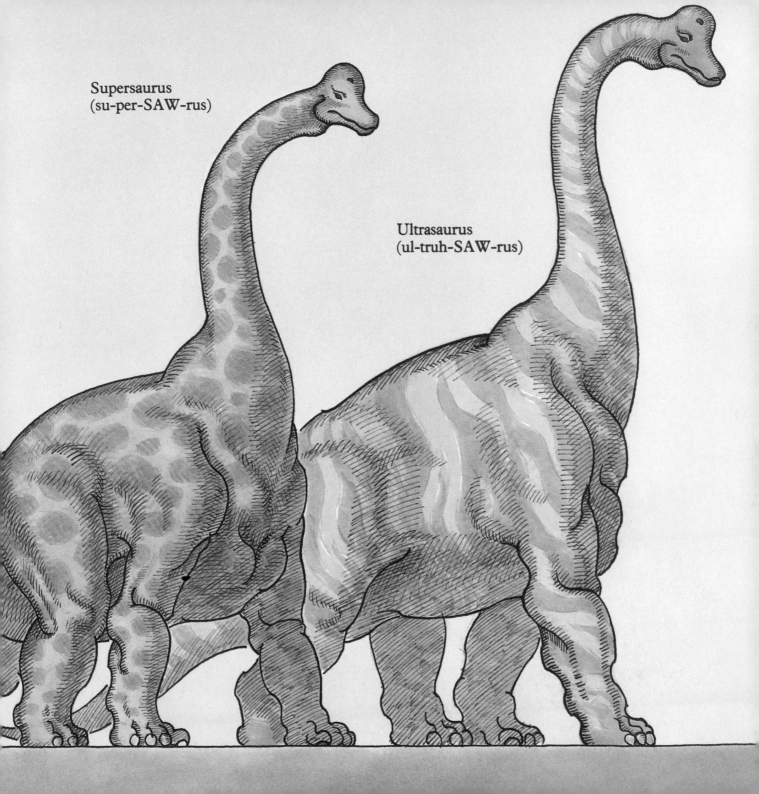

Supersaurus
(su-per-SAW-rus)

Ultrasaurus
(ul-truh-SAW-rus)

Ultrasaurus was so big that it made most other dinosaurs look small. It stood 60 feet tall and was 100 feet long.

Scientists found the bones of Ultrasaurus in a
desert in the western part of the United States.

The scientists found only the Ultrasaurus' leg bones. They used these bones to determine how big the dinosaur was.

This is what scientists think a whole
Ultrasaurus skeleton looked like.
   Was Ultrasaurus the biggest dinosaur of
all? Maybe not.

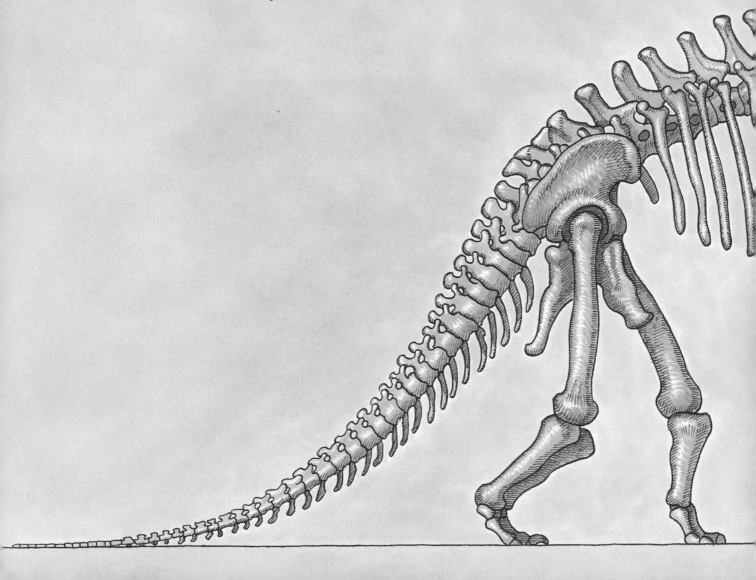

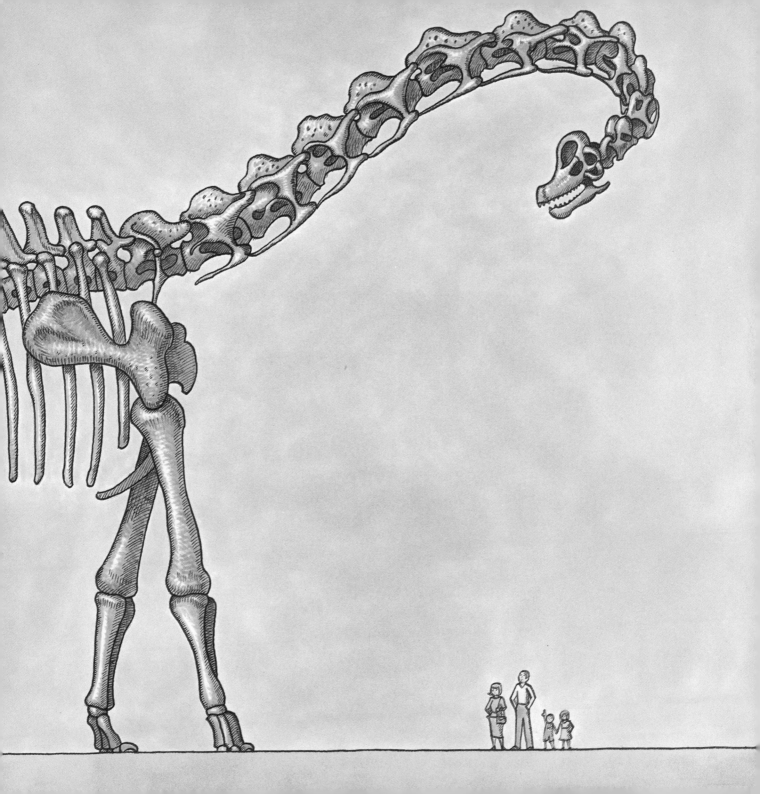

Recently the bones of another giant dinosaur called Seismosaurus (size-mo-SAW-rus) were discovered in New Mexico. It may have been the biggest creature ever to walk on Earth. Could there have been even *bigger* dinosaurs?

Perhaps their bones are waiting to be found deep in the earth. Maybe someday *you* might be the one to find them.